# War Eagle!

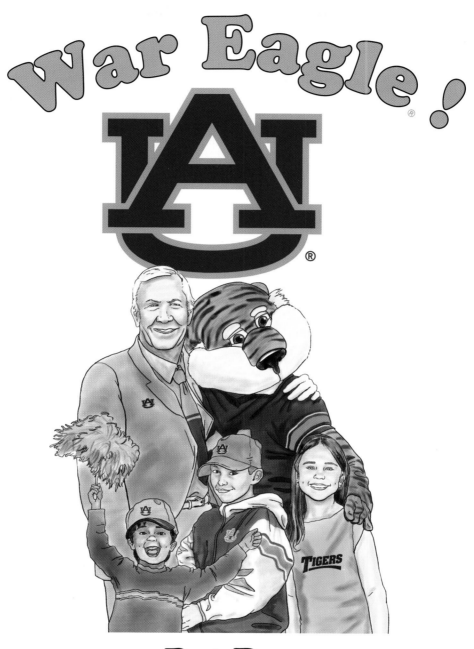

## Pat Dye

### Illustrated by Miguel De Angel

www.mascotbooks.com

It was football season again
at Auburn University. Aubie was on his
way to Jordan-Hare Stadium.

On campus, he met a group
of fans near the library.
The fans cheered, "War Eagle!"

At the stadium, Aubie ran into friendly tailgaters that had gathered for the big game.

As the tailgaters enjoyed a cookout,
they cheered, "War Eagle!"

It was now time for the Tiger Walk. Aubie led thousands of fans as they cheered wildly for the football team.

As the players walked by,
the crowd cheered, "War Eagle!"

Aubie joined the football team in the
locker room before the big game.

The coach gave the team final
instructions and cheered, "War Eagle!"

Inside the stadium, Aubie watched
as the golden eagle soared
high above the field.

The crowd cheered, "War Eagle!"

Aubie and the football team ran out of
the tunnel, through the smoke,
and onto Pat Dye Field.

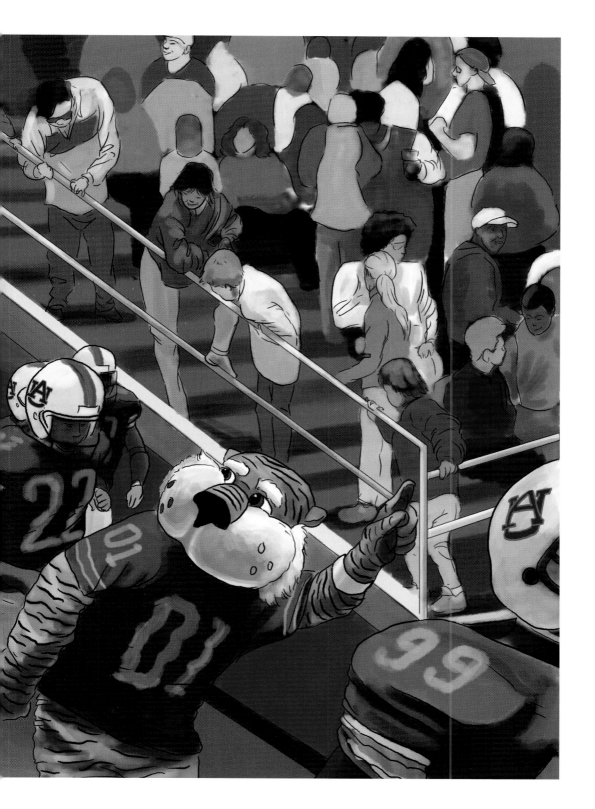

A tiger roar could be heard
throughout the stadium.
The players cheered, "War Eagle!"

After the Tigers scored a touchdown,
Aubie performed a touchdown dance.

The crowd was amazed by Aubie's summersault. Everybody laughed and cheered, "War Eagle!"

At halftime, Aubie joined the
Auburn Band as they
marched into formation.

After a great performance,
the band cheered, "War Eagle!"

It was now time for a cheer. One side of the stadium cheered, "AUBURN!" then the other side cheered, "TIGERS!"

Aubie went into the stands to greet
some of his friends.
His friends said, "War Eagle!"

As the game ended,
Auburn fans celebrated the victory
by singing the War Eagle fight song.

The crowd cheered,
"War Eagle fearless and true,
fight on you orange and blue!"

After the game, Aubie joined
many happy Auburn fans for the
traditional rolling of Toomer's Corner.

It was a great way to end the
perfect day at Auburn University.
Everyone cheered, "War Eagle!"

This book is dedicated to the youngest
Auburn fans, a big part of the Auburn family.
I hope that this little book will be a reminder
to them just how special Auburn really is.
Remember, "It's great to be an Auburn Tiger!"

~ Coach Pat Dye

For Sue, Ana Milagros, and Angel Miguel ~ Miguel De Angel

For more information about our products,
please visit us online at www.mascotbooks.com.

For more information, please contact Mascot Books,
P.O. Box 220157, Chantilly, VA 20153-0157

ISBN: 1-932888-47-0

Printed in the United States.